Lemonade Stand

Written and Illustrated by Dee Smith

Copyright © 2016

Visit Deesignery.com

WITHDRAWN
FROM THE RECORDS OF THE
MID-CONTINENT PUBLIC LIBRARY

It's summer time and the air is hot.

Go find the perfect treat.

I know the perfect spot.

The lemonade stand waits just for you.

Go to the lemonade stand.

You will know what to do!

Go up to the counter, smile and order your drink.

You'll be happy once your lips touch the cup's tilted brink.

It's yellow, frosty and perfection in every way.

It's a wonderful treat on a hot
summer day.

The ice will spin and clink around in your cup.

You'll hurry to drink this tasty chilled drink up.

One sip of lemonade simply won't do.

You'll want to drink up all of this cold summer stew.

Fresh lemon juice has been mixed with sugar water with care.

The yellow drink glitters and looks like gold over there.

There's the lemonade stand.

You know what to do.

Get a cup of fresh lemonade.

One for me and one for you!

More Books from Bee-Ville

What to Bee?- **A rhyming picture book about good virtues, values and behavior.**

Are you Bee-ing Bullied?- **A rhyming picture book about what to do if you are being bullied.**

Thank You!

Thank you so much for reading this book.
It means the world to me!
If you liked the book I would much appreciate if you would write a Review on Amazon. I am so thankful for each and every person supporting my dream of being a writer for children. Because you have read this book, yes that means YOU too! Thanks Again!
Stay tuned for more titles on my website Deesignery.com

Regards,
Dee

About the Author:

My name is Dee Smith. I am an Author and Illustrator. My hobbies include graphic design, puppetry, balloon twisting, drawing and of course writing. I am dedicated to my mission of keeping children entertained in fun and innovative ways.

Made in the USA
Coppell, TX
11 June 2021

57262458R00017